W9-BFR-700

The Upside-Down Reader

By Wilhelm Gruber
Illustrated by Marlies Rieper-Bastian

Translated by J. Alison James

North-South Books
NEW YORK / LONDON

First published in the United States, Great Britain, Canada,
Australia, and New Zealand in 1998 by North-South Books,
an imprint of Nord-Süd Verlag AG, Gossau Zürich, Switzerland.

Distributed in the United States by North-South Books Inc., New York.

Library of Congress Cataloging-in-Publication Data is available.
ISBN 1-55858-974-0 (TRADE BINDING)
ISBN 1-55858-975-9 (LIBRARY BINDING)

A CIP catalogue record for this book
is available from The British Library.

1 3 5 7 9 TB 10 8 6 4 2
1 3 5 7 9 LB 10 8 6 4 2
Printed in Belgium

Contents

Tina Goes to School

Before Mother came to get Tim at playschool, she picked up his big sister Tina.

It was Tina's first week at school. She had a bright new backpack for her books.

After Tina and Mother picked up Tim, they all walked home together.

Tina talked about school. She talked about the teachers; she talked about the children.

Tim listened.

Tina let him wear the backpack. He needed to get used to it, since next year he was going to go to school too. But soon Tina asked for her backpack again. She was the one in *real* school. Not Tim.

"Come to the table," called Mother.
Lunch was spaghetti and meatballs.

After lunch, Tina unpacked her
backpack.

Tim watched.

"You can't sit there," said Tina.

"Why not?" asked Tim.

"Because I need to study."

"Tina has to do her homework,"
explained Mother.

Tim argued, "But why can't I sit next to her?"

"Because it bothers me!" Tina said.

Tim tried one last time: "But I can learn too."

"You can learn to go away," said Tina.

Tim went sadly to his room.

Family Talk

We'll talk to Dad about it when he gets home, thought Tim. That's what Mother always does when there is a problem.

Tim played with the pirate ship. He shot the cannons. But he had to bring the cannonballs back himself. How boring.

He went outside to wait for Dad. He
wanted a chance to tell him everything
before Tina messed things up.

Finally Dad came! He'd gone shopping
after work. Tim took a box.

"Dad . . . ?" asked Tim.

But Dad had his hands full. "Not right now, Tim. Could you please open the door?"

It wasn't until suppertime that they
were able to have the talk.

"Does he really bother you, Tina?"
asked Dad.

Mother gave him a look. "Of course he
does. He sits right next to her," she said.

Dad thought for a moment. "Well,
maybe not right at her side." He scratched
his chin. "How about if you sat in my
place, right across from her?"

Dad looked at Tim. "And you must promise to be quiet and not bother her."

Mother said, "We'll give you paper and crayons. If you're drawing, you won't be a bother."

"Okay," said Tim happily.

Tina nodded too.

"All right," said Mother. "Let's try it."

Green Grass

The next day, Tim sat in Dad's place, right across the table. Tina took out her reader and showed Mother her new words.

Tim drew blue clouds and a yellow sun in the corner. He peeked at the reader.

Tina put her finger under the words. Tim followed her finger with his eyes. When Tina looked up, Tim drew grass. "P e t e," read Tina slowly.

Tim watched to see exactly which word she was pointing to. "P e t e," he said to himself. Next to the word was a picture of Pete. For Tim, Pete was standing on his head.

Soon Tina could read entire sentences.

Pat and Pete draw.

Her finger ran under the words. Across the table, Tim paid close attention. Word for word, he read along:

Pat and Pete draw.

Every day there was a new page. And along with Tina, Tim learned all the new words. But for him the page was always turned around.

Whenever Tina looked up, Tim busily drew the sun, clouds, and lots of green grass.

If Tina left the room, Tim turned the book around and looked at the pictures. With his finger, he ran along under the words. But this way they looked completely different. Tim didn't understand a word.

When he turned the book back upside down, he could understand everything.

He began from the bottom and went to the top, reading along from right to left.

Pat	Pete	Sam	ball

Pat, Pete, and Sam play in the yard.
They throw the ball.
Throw the ball to Pete, Pat!

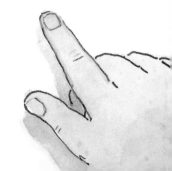

When Tim and his mother went shopping one afternoon, they went past a newspaper stand. Tim took down one magazine after another and looked at the pictures. Then he turned them upside down to read the words. When he put them away, they were still upside down.

The man at the newspaper stand shook his head, and turned them back right side up.

Tim Tries to Do a Headstand

After a while, Tina could read a lot of pages. Tim drew so many meadows that the green crayon was a stub.

One day, Tina and Tim took a walk.
Tina read a sign, then laughed.

"What are you laughing at?" Tim asked.
"What does it say?"

"I'm not telling," said Tina.

Tim turned his head sideways, but he
could not read the letters.

"You're horrible," he cried.

Tim tried a headstand. But he fell down.
What did it say that made Tina laugh?

Do Letters Have Heads?

One day Tina couldn't figure out a word in her reading book. She stopped.

Tim looked closely and said the word aloud.

"Tim's bothering me!" cried Tina.

"I am not!" Tim said. "I'm only helping her read."

"You can read it better than Tina?" asked Mother.

Tina answered for him. "Of course not!"

"Yes I can!" he cried.

Tina couldn't stand for that. She turned
her book around and shoved it under Tim's
nose. "Go ahead," she said. "Show me."

Tim turned back a few pages and read,
"Pat and Pete paint."

"Anyone could do that," said Tina.
"That is at the very beginning. Tim knows
the pictures. And he remembers which
words go with them. That isn't reading!"

Tina flipped to the back of the book.

"Now try reading a page without pictures!"

Tim turned the book around so it faced the way it did when Tina read. Then he read, from bottom to top, from right to left: "W h e r e   i s   t h e   b a l l ? T h e   b a l l   i s   o n   t h e   r o o f."

"Stop, you're faking!" cried Tina.

"I am not! I'm reading!"

Mother put down the watering can and came over to see what Tim was doing.

"You've turned the book the wrong way."

"Why is it wrong?" asked Tim. "I can hold the book any way I want."

"But the letters are all standing on their heads," she explained.

"Letters don't have heads," said Tim.

At the Station

Grandma Lisa was coming for a visit.
Tim and Tina helped clean the house.
Then Tim made a sign that said "I love
you, Grandma!" for the front door.

"Who's coming along to the station?"
Dad asked.

Everyone wanted to come.

"Wait!" cried Tim. "The sign!"

Everyone waited while Tim quickly
stuck the sign on the door of the house.

At the station, they had to wait. The
train was late.

Dad looked at the train timetable.
It listed all the cities where the train
would stop before it came here.

43

"Grandma Lisa is coming from Bristol.
Where else does the train go?" asked Dad.

"Ask Tim," said Tina. "He thinks he
can read."

Tim looked up at the timetable.

"Why don't you just turn it upside down?" asked Tina, grinning.

Tim didn't know what to do at first. Then he got an idea. He threw his jacket on the ground by a post. Then he bent over, tucked his head in, stuck out his hands, kicked up, and leaned his feet against the post. He did it! A headstand!

45

That was what he'd been learning in playschool all this time. Tim sounded out all the names of all the towns on the board one after the other.

Then he fell down.

Dad was astonished. "You really can read!"

"But only upside down," said Tina.

Mother looked amazed.

Just then the train pulled up and Grandma Lisa arrived.

Automat Land

At home Tim's sign hung on the door.
Grandma Lisa smiled when she tried to
read the upside-down writing. The first
thing she did when she got inside was get
out presents. For Tim she'd brought a
drawing pad and crayons. Tim smiled.
There was a new green one. For Tina she
had brought a book called *The Children
from Automat Land*.

"Now that you are learning to read," she said.

"Thank you, Grandma," said Tina, and she leafed through the book. Then she put it down.

When Tina wasn't looking, Tim opened the book. He started to read it.

Grandma looked surprised. "Wouldn't you rather read it the other way around?" she asked. "This way the writing is upside down! Like the sign on the door."

Tim was embarrassed. He shut the book.

After supper, Tina took the new book and read aloud to Grandma. Tim sat across from her. Tina read, "Automat Land is a very strange land. Everything goes by itself. In school, the children have . . ." The next words were long. Tina tried it again quietly. ". . . In school, the children have . . . have . . ."

". . . automatic pencil sharpeners with a propeller drive and a remote control," read Tim.

Tina looked at him angrily.

"Do you know this book?" Grandma Lisa asked Tim.

Tim shook his head.

"So how do you know what is written there?"

Tim shrugged his shoulders.

"Where did you see those words? Show me."

"There," said Tim. He ran his finger over the words "automatic pencil sharpeners with a propeller drive and a remote control."

"But that's the wrong way to read," said Grandma.

Tim was embarrassed. He felt like crying. He liked to read, but everybody told him he was doing it wrong.

AUTOMAT LAND!

Upside-Down Reader

Grandma Lisa called to Tim. "Here, I got you your own reading book." Then she drew heads and feet on all the pages. "Now you'll always know," she said, "which is the top and which is the bottom. And the more I read to you right side up, the more you'll understand words this way."

"Really?" asked Tim.

"Really," said Grandma Lisa.

Tina looked sad.

Quickly Grandma said, "We can put feet and a head on Tina's reader as well. That way everyone will know what side is up."

Tina and Tim sat down side by side in their own seats at the table. Tina had a new book, and so did Tim.

Grandma Lisa quietly whispered the words to Tim as he traced his finger, from left to right, from top to bottom.

Soon the funny-looking letters became words, and the words became stories.

He was reading right side up!

"Looks like we've got two new readers," said Mother. "What shall we do to celebrate?"

"Let's have Grandma's automatic apple cake!" cried Tim.

"Oh, there is nothing automatic about that," said Dad. "It's a lot of hard work."

"Everything takes time and practice," said Grandma. "Do you have any apples?"

Tina said to Tim, "Now we can read to each other. We won't have to wait for Mother or Dad to hear a story!" She smiled at Tim. "I'm glad you can read just like me," she said.

"Really?" Tim said. Then he grinned. "Me too!"

About the Author

Wilhelm Gruber was born in a small town in Germany. As a child, his favorite things to do were play soccer, build treehouses, and fish. He now lives with his family in Muenster, where he teaches reading at a school for learning-disabled children. This is his first book for North-South.

About the Illustrator

Marlies Rieper-Bastian was born in Germany. She has worked as a graphic designer in advertising and has illustrated numerous textbooks and picture books for children. She now lives in Braunschweig, Germany. This is her first book for North-South.

Other North-South Easy-to-Read Books